MENTAL HEALTH GUIDES

UNDERSTANDING
SUICIDAL
FEELINGS

by R. L. Van

BrightPoint Press

San Diego, CA

© 2022 BrightPoint Press
an imprint of ReferencePoint Press, Inc.
Printed in the United States

For more information, contact:
BrightPoint Press
PO Box 27779
San Diego, CA 92198
www.BrightPointPress.com

ALL RIGHTS RESERVED.

No part of this work covered by the copyright hereon may be reproduced or used in any form or by any means—graphic, electronic, or mechanical, including photocopying, recording, taping, web distribution, or information storage retrieval systems—without the written permission of the publisher.

Content Consultant: Keyne C. Law, PhD, Assistant Professor of Clinical Psychology, Seattle Pacific University

---

LIBRARY OF CONGRESS CATALOGING-IN-PUBLICATION DATA

Names: Van, R. L., author.
Title: Understanding suicidal feelings / R. L. Van.
Description: San Diego, CA : BrightPoint Press, 2022. | Series: Mental health guides | Includes bibliographical references and index. | Audience: Grades 7-9
Identifiers: LCCN 2021002772 (print) | LCCN 2021002773 (eBook) | ISBN 9781678201449 (hardcover) | ISBN 9781678201456 (eBook)
Subjects: LCSH: Suicide--Psychological aspects--Juvenile literature. | Suicidal behavior--Juvenile literature. | Emotions--Juvenile literature.
Classification: LCC HV6545 .V296 2022 (print) | LCC HV6545 (eBook) | DDC 616.85/8445--dc23
LC record available at https://lccn.loc.gov/2021002772
LC eBook record available at https://lccn.loc.gov/2021002773

CONTENTS

Content Warning: This book describes suicide and suicidal thoughts, which may be triggering to some readers.

AT A GLANCE	**4**
INTRODUCTION	**6**
EXPERIENCING SUICIDAL FEELINGS	
CHAPTER ONE	**14**
WHAT ARE SUICIDAL FEELINGS?	
CHAPTER TWO	**30**
HOW DO SUICIDAL FEELINGS AFFECT PEOPLE?	
CHAPTER THREE	**44**
HOW DO SUICIDAL FEELINGS AFFECT SOCIETY?	
CHAPTER FOUR	**58**
HOW ARE SUICIDAL FEELINGS TREATED?	
Glossary	74
Source Notes	75
For Further Research	76
Index	78
Image Credits	79
About the Author	80

AT A GLANCE

- Suicidal thoughts affect many people in the United States each year, including children and teens. Suicide is the second leading cause of death in people ages ten to twenty-four.

- Mental health conditions, life events, and other factors may worsen suicidal thoughts.

- Suicidal thoughts and urges often have other symptoms. People may talk about dying, lose interest in things, or experience other changes.

- Moments when people experience extreme suicidal urges are difficult but temporary. Many people who are about to attempt suicide find that this urge goes away in a short time.

- Populations are affected by suicide at different rates. People in certain communities, such as Native populations and LGBTQ people, may be at a higher risk of dying by suicide.

- Society has a negative attitude toward suicide that may prevent people from talking about it. This can make those experiencing suicidal thoughts and those who have lost a loved one to suicide less likely to seek support.

- There are many treatments available to lessen suicidal thoughts. These include cognitive behavioral therapy and dialectical behavior therapy, medications, and other types of treatments.

- Lifestyle changes, healthy relationships, and access to mental health care can reduce a person's risk of suicide.

INTRODUCTION

EXPERIENCING SUICIDAL FEELINGS

Jayden felt alone. His friends didn't seem to want to spend time with him. They had avoided him since his mom died in a car accident. Jayden thought they only talked to him because they felt like they had to. He felt like a burden.

Someone who is thinking about suicide may lose interest in things he or she previously enjoyed.

Jayden played soccer. He used to really like it. And he used to love reading. But lately he didn't enjoy those things. He felt worthless and trapped. The pain of these feelings seemed unbearable.

He began to think about ending his life. He had watched TV shows where people killed themselves. He began to look up ways to do this.

One day his friend Gina asked him what was wrong. He told her he felt like he didn't have a reason to live. She asked him if he was considering suicide. Jayden was relieved to finally have someone to talk to. He said he was thinking about it. Gina hugged him. She said that things would get better.

A person should always tell an adult about a friend's suicidal thoughts and urges.

Jayden asked her not to tell anyone.

But Gina said she had to tell an adult.

They decided to go see the school counselor together.

Having a strong support system is helpful for those dealing with suicidal thoughts.

The counselor told Jayden his pain was temporary. She reminded him that people cared about him. Jayden went home and told his dad what he'd been thinking. His dad told him how much he loved him.

Soon, Jayden began seeing a therapist. They worked together on dealing with his suicidal thinking. Jayden learned ways to cope. His doctor also prescribed him an antidepressant. After a while, he started to enjoy reading and soccer again. He started telling some friends what he was going through. Most of them didn't treat him any differently. They were all glad he was getting help.

Sometimes Jayden still felt sad. But he focused on the people who loved him. He didn't feel worthless anymore. He wanted to keep living.

WHAT IS SUICIDE?

Jayden is a fictional character. But his experience with suicidal thoughts is not uncommon. Suicide is when a person ends his or her own life on purpose. Unfortunately, many people attempt suicide. In 2018, 1.4 million people in the United States attempted suicide. More

Support groups can help people who are experiencing suicidal thoughts.

than 48,000 people died by suicide that year. Suicide is the tenth most common cause of death. And it is the second most common cause of death in people ages ten to twenty-four. Fortunately, there are treatments available. These treatments can help address suicide and suicidal thoughts.

CHAPTER ONE

WHAT ARE SUICIDAL FEELINGS?

People who have suicidal thoughts think about killing themselves. They may feel there is no hope for solving their problems. They may think they are a burden to their family and friends. They may withdraw from others. Some people may experience suicidal thoughts for a very long

Someone experiencing suicidal thoughts may not believe that things will get better.

time. Others may have these thoughts only during an especially difficult time.

There are many risk factors for suicide and suicidal thoughts. Having a mental health condition greatly increases the chance of suicidal thoughts. Challenges in daily life may also increase suicidal thoughts. Difficulties coping with **trauma** or stress are risk factors. Suicide risk increases with multiple risk factors.

MENTAL HEALTH CONDITIONS AND SUICIDAL FEELINGS

Having a mental health condition does not mean someone will attempt suicide. He or she may not experience suicidal thoughts. Most people who have a mental illness do not die by suicide. They are able to live fulfilling lives. Similarly, not everyone who dies by suicide has a mental health condition. However, many types of mental illnesses can increase the risk of suicide.

These conditions are treatable. Proper treatment can lessen suicidal thoughts.

Many people who die by suicide may have an undiagnosed mental condition. Dr. Jill Harkavy-Friedman researches suicidal behavior at Columbia University.

SUICIDE PREVENTION HOTLINES

There are many ways to get help for suicidal thoughts. Resources include suicide prevention hotlines. These are crisis centers people can call, text, or chat with online. They help people who are thinking about suicide. Trained crisis counselors offer support around the clock. One US hotline is the National Suicide Prevention Lifeline. Its phone number is 1-800-273-8255. Its Lifeline Chat is available at suicidepreventionlifeline.org/chat.

She said "[About] 90 percent of people who died by suicide had a diagnosable . . . mental health condition at the time of their death."[1]

Depression, or major depressive disorder, is a mental health condition. Suicidal thoughts are symptoms of depression. People with depression may be unable to imagine being happy. They may believe that suicide is the only way to end their emotional pain. Treating depression can reduce suicidal thoughts.

Bipolar disorders also may contribute to suicidal thoughts. People with a bipolar

Certain mental health conditions, such as depression, can put someone at a higher risk of having suicidal thoughts.

disorder experience periods of high energy and excitement. They also experience periods of depression. Treating bipolar disorder **stabilizes** a person's mood. This helps prevent depressive episodes and suicidal thoughts.

Another mental disorder connected to suicide is schizophrenia. About 10 percent of people with schizophrenia die by suicide. This illness affects people's thoughts, behaviors, and emotions. It can cause people to believe things that are not true. Some people sense things that are not there. They may hear voices. These voices may tell a person to harm or even kill himself. Schizophrenia can be treated. Treatment can reduce the risk of suicide.

Other mental health conditions increase the risk of suicide. Post-traumatic stress disorder (PTSD) is connected to

Doctors may give a person medication to treat a mental health condition.

suicidal thoughts. Eating disorders and other conditions can also contribute to suicidal thoughts.

SUBSTANCE USE AND SUICIDE

Substance use disorders are mental health conditions. People with substance use disorders abuse alcohol or drugs.

Substance use is a major risk factor for suicide. Substance use and suicidal thoughts may come from the same root cause. People may abuse substances to self-medicate. They want a temporary escape from negative feelings. Substance use disorders are treatable. These treatments help people address stress in a positive way. They reduce a person's use of a substance. And they lessen suicidal thinking.

Alcohol use has strong connections to suicide. Twenty-two percent of suicides in the United States involve alcohol

Alcohol is a factor in many suicides.

intoxication. Alcohol is a factor in up to 40 percent of suicide attempts. Other drugs are also present in a significant number of suicides.

Substance use and suicide are related for a few reasons. Substance use can reduce self-control. It can increase impulsive behavior. Alcohol worsens a person's depressed mood. It can affect a person's thinking.

LIFE EVENTS AND SUICIDAL FEELINGS

Trauma is another risk factor for suicidal thoughts. Trauma includes abuse, sexual assault, and car accidents. It can also be things like the death of a loved one or going to war. Other stressful life events can increase the risk of suicidal urges too.

A traumatic event, such as a car crash, may trigger suicidal feelings.

These could be things like a breakup or learning about another person's suicide.

A woman named Kristin Rivas attempted suicide after trauma. Her sister had died in a car accident. Then her fiancé called off their wedding. She says, "My thoughts told me I was broken . . . that I could never be happy, hopeful, or love again. I felt so much . . . pain all at once. I couldn't stand it one second longer."[2] Now, Rivas works with others who are experiencing suicidal urges. She helps them get relief from suicidal thoughts.

A family history of suicide can lead to suicidal thoughts. Previous suicide attempts are also a risk factor. People who have previously attempted suicide are more likely to have suicidal thoughts. They are also more likely to attempt suicide again. But that doesn't mean everyone who survives a suicide attempt will die by suicide later. Ninety percent of suicide attempt survivors do not die by another suicide attempt.

Life challenges can also be risk factors for suicidal thoughts. Bullying and harassment are causes of ongoing stress. So is struggling with relationships, money,

FIREARMS AND RISK OF SUICIDE

Having access to firearms is a risk factor for suicide. People who have easy access to a firearm are at a much higher risk of dying by suicide. This is because firearms are extremely lethal. Other methods of suicide allow people time to reconsider during an attempt. In the United States, states with many gun owners have much higher suicide rates than states with fewer gun owners.

or health. People who feel alone are at greater risk of suicidal thoughts.

SUICIDAL FEELINGS AND THE BRAIN

Studies have found possible connections between the brain and suicidal urges. One study looked at the brains of people who died by suicide. It found low levels of the **neurotransmitter** serotonin. This chemical helps regulate mood.

Suicidal urges may also be connected to differences in some areas of the brain. One study compared the brains of people with depression. One group had attempted suicide, and the other had not. Those

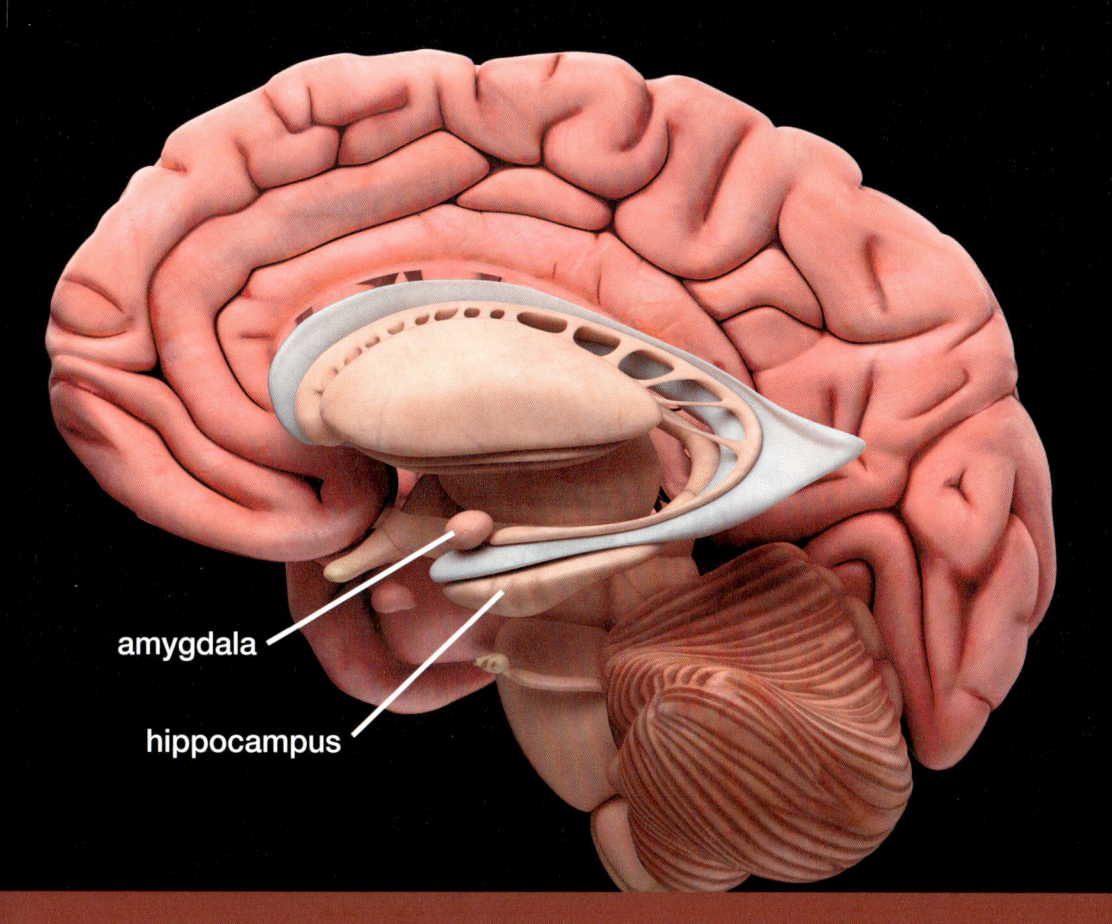

Studies have found that some parts of the brain are smaller in people who have attempted suicide.

who had attempted suicide had a smaller hippocampus. Another study found the amygdalae were also smaller in those with suicide attempts. Both of these are parts of the brain that respond to stress.

CHAPTER TWO

HOW DO SUICIDAL FEELINGS AFFECT PEOPLE?

People experience suicidal thoughts in different ways. And a person's thoughts can change from moment to moment. Many people who have suicidal thoughts often think about killing themselves. They may plan a suicide

Someone experiencing suicidal thoughts may think about death often.

attempt. But there are other symptoms that can come with suicidal thoughts.

Some people with suicidal thoughts stop caring about their appearances. They may stop grooming or cleaning themselves.

They may cry often and feel unbearable emotional pain. Those who feel this way may believe death is the only way to end their suffering. Others may think life is not worth living.

A woman named Kelley Clink attempted suicide when she was sixteen. She survived. She says she loves her life now. She wants to keep living. She described the suicidal thoughts she experienced. She said, "There was a voice in my head telling me I was worthless. It said no one loved me. That I was weak. Sick. Broken. Wrong. It said I didn't belong. . . . It told me I was

Sleep patterns may change when someone is experiencing suicidal thoughts.

a burden on the people I loved. . . . And it was so loud I couldn't hear anything else."[3]

Suicidal thoughts can come with physical symptoms too. People may sleep too much or too little. They may feel numb or disconnected from their bodies. Their appetite or weight may change.

SELF-HARM AND STIGMA

People experiencing suicidal thoughts may self-harm. This is when people hurt themselves intentionally. There are many reasons people self-harm. Some do it because they believe it can control their emotions. They may be trying to distract themselves from their emotional pain. People who self-harm may not be trying to die. But self-harm is dangerous. It can cause serious injury and even accidental death. It can worsen emotional and mental health issues. And it increases the risk of suicidal thoughts and behaviors.

Stigma may prevent people from talking about their suicidal thoughts. There is a lot of stigma around suicide and mental health. A suicidal person may feel ashamed or

> **TALKING ABOUT SUICIDE**
>
> Lady Gaga is a famous singer. She is open about her struggles with PTSD and suicidal thoughts. She started an organization called the Born This Way Foundation. It works with young people to start conversations about mental health and end stigma around it. The foundation helped start the Teen Mental Health First Aid program. It teaches teens about mental health conditions. It trains them to help friends who are struggling.

Discussion of suicide or suicidal thoughts should always be taken seriously.

guilty because of this stigma. Other people may hold negative stereotypes about suicide. They may be judgmental instead of supportive. This stigma can isolate people experiencing suicidal thoughts. It may prevent them from getting help.

WARNING SIGNS

Many people experiencing suicidal urges change their behavior. Nearly 80 percent of people who attempt suicide show warning signs beforehand. But there will not always be warning signs for a suicide.

A person experiencing suicidal thoughts may talk about wanting to die. Some people research ways to kill themselves. They may buy a weapon. Some people write or talk about dying often. People with suicidal urges may start doing risky things. These can include substance use or other dangerous activities.

Another change in behavior may be emotional. It's important to watch for sadness and depression. But other emotions can be signs of suicidal thoughts. A person may act anxious, agitated, or irritable. They might have extreme mood swings. They might seem angry and talk about revenge. Or their emotions may suddenly improve. This may be because they have decided to end their own lives and feel relieved.

People who plan to attempt suicide may give away their belongings. They may suddenly return things they have borrowed.

Someone who is considering suicide may suddenly reach out to say goodbye.

They may visit or call people to reconnect or to say goodbye.

Any warning sign of suicide should be taken seriously. A person should speak up if they notice someone showing warning signs. They should ask the person if they are considering suicide. They may share resources with the person who is feeling suicidal. They should offer support and friendship. These small steps can make a difference.

It is also important to tell an adult as soon as possible. A friend may ask for their suicidal thoughts to be kept a secret. But telling an adult is the safest thing to do if someone is suicidal.

UNDERSTANDING SUICIDE ATTEMPTS

Some people may not understand how someone reaches the point of considering suicide. Sometimes people

Someone experiencing suicidal feelings may feel intense emotional pain.

who attempt suicide are in a particular mindset. They are unable to come up with solutions to problems. They feel like things can't change.

Dr. Stacey Freedenthal is a therapist. She explained what being in this mindset is like. She said, "I've heard it described as a mental toothache. If you have a toothache, all you can think about is the pain in your tooth. And combine that with the [belief] that this pain will never end."[4]

But this mindset is not permanent. Nearly half of people who attempted suicide considered it less than twenty minutes beforehand. If a person waits, this suicidal moment may end.

Suicide survivors may experience other effects. They may suffer injuries. These include things like broken bones and brain injuries. Some injuries cause long-term health issues. Attempting suicide can also contribute to depression and other mental health conditions.

SURVIVING A SUICIDE ATTEMPT

A man name Kevin Hines attempted suicide in 2000. He jumped off the Golden Gate Bridge in San Francisco, California. He suffered severe injuries. But he survived. A sea lion kept him afloat. Afterward, Hines devoted his life to preventing suicide. He teaches people about wellness and mental health. He also fought for a safety net to be built at the Golden Gate Bridge. He succeeded. Construction on the safety net began in 2017.

CHAPTER THREE

HOW DO SUICIDAL FEELINGS AFFECT SOCIETY?

Anyone can experience suicidal thoughts. But people in certain groups may be at a higher risk. Suicide rates differ across races. They also vary by gender, age, and sexuality.

Native populations have a high risk of suicide.

Native populations have the highest suicide rate in the United States. White people have the second-highest rate. Black, Hispanic, and Asian and Pacific Islander populations all have much lower rates. The rates of suicidal thoughts do not differ as much across racial groups in youth. But Native adults are at a higher risk for suicidal thoughts.

People of different races may attempt suicide for different reasons. Latinos are more likely to be influenced by outside issues. These include job loss and discrimination. White people are more likely to be influenced by internal issues such as feeling hopeless.

Suicide risk also varies by age. People forty-five to sixty-four years old have the highest rate of suicide. People fifteen to twenty-four have a lower suicide rate than

Job loss can trigger suicidal thoughts.

older adults. But young adults have higher rates of suicidal thoughts. They are also more likely to attempt suicide.

Women are at a higher risk for suicide attempts than men. But men have a higher rate of suicide. In 2018, the suicide rate for men was 3.7 times the rate for women.

This is partly because men are more likely to use firearms in suicide attempts.

People in certain careers are at higher risk of suicide. One major risk factor is time spent in the military. Veterans are 1.5 times more likely to die by suicide than nonveterans are.

LGBTQ IDENTITIES AND SUICIDE

LGBTQ youth have a high risk of suicide. **Transgender** youth are at a very high risk. A 2020 survey looked at this risk. More than half of transgender youth had seriously considered suicide in the past year. Over 60 percent reported self-harm behaviors.

SUICIDAL THOUGHTS AND URGES IN HIGH SCHOOL STUDENTS IN 2019

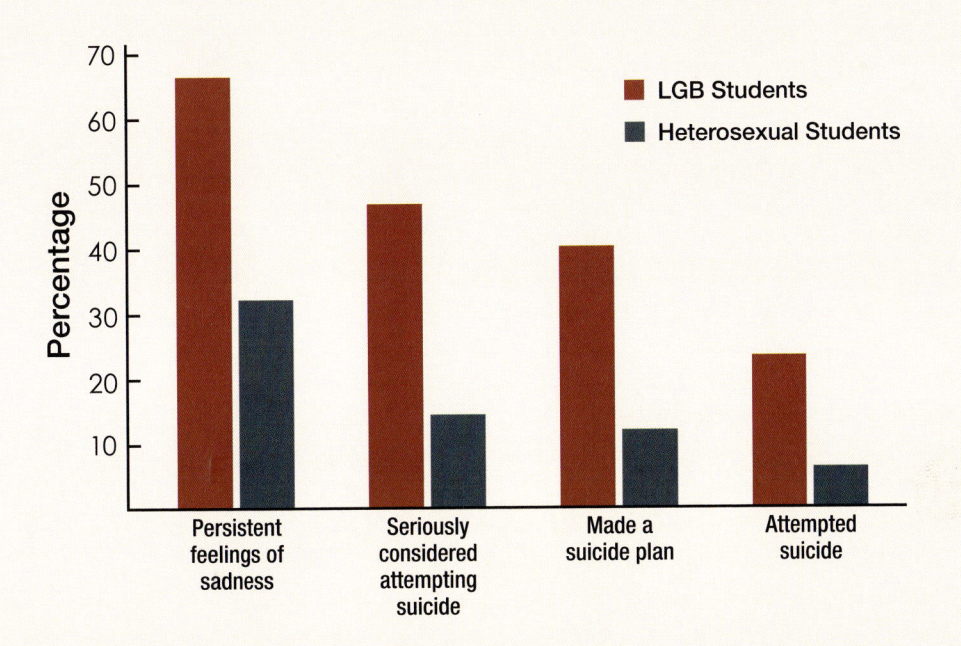

[Bar chart showing percentages for LGB Students vs Heterosexual Students across four categories:
- Persistent feelings of sadness: LGB ~66%, Heterosexual ~32%
- Seriously considered attempting suicide: LGB ~47%, Heterosexual ~15%
- Made a suicide plan: LGB ~41%, Heterosexual ~13%
- Attempted suicide: LGB ~24%, Heterosexual ~7%]

Source: Michelle M. Johns, et al, "Trends in Violence Victimization and Suicide Risk by Sexual Identity Among High School Students—Youth Risk Behavior Survey, United States, 2015–2019," CDC, August 21, 2019. www.cdc.gov.

Lesbian, gay, or bisexual (LGB) high school students experience suicidal thoughts and urges at higher rates than heterosexual students.

LGBTQ youth may face rejection and violence. These experiences increase the risk of attempting suicide. Dr. Jack Turban works in child and adolescent psychiatry at Stanford University. He said, "We can't underestimate the . . . health effects caused by societal discrimination against LGBTQ people."[5]

Support can make a big difference. LGBTQ students attending schools with

LGBTQ SUICIDE PREVENTION

There are many resources for LGBTQ people experiencing suicidal thoughts. The Trevor Project is one. It offers suicide prevention resources for LGBTQ youth. These include a hotline, chat and text support, and more. Another organization is the It Gets Better Project. The project connects LGBTQ youth around the world with stories of hope. It works to empower them and provide help when needed.

Schools that include safe spaces for LGBTQ students help lower suicide risk in these students.

gay-straight alliances are less likely to attempt suicide. Respecting LGBTQ identities lowers suicide risk.

STIGMA

There is a lot of stigma around suicide. People may say that someone "committed suicide." This language suggests the person has committed a crime. It increases the negative views of people who attempt suicide.

Some myths about suicide increase stigma. Some people may think attempting suicide is weak or cowardly. They may believe that people attempt suicide for attention. These myths are not true. They can even be dangerous. They may prevent a suicidal person from seeking help. These myths may also prevent others from taking the person's feelings seriously.

SUICIDAL FEELINGS AND CULTURE

People in different cultures may respond to suicidal thoughts differently. One study surveyed college students. It found that students of color were less likely to seek help for suicidal thoughts. Some cultures

SUICIDE IN THE MEDIA

The portrayal of suicide in media may be connected to viewers' suicidal thoughts. One study had adults watch movies with different endings. One movie ended in a suicide. Adults already experiencing suicidal thoughts had an increase in these thoughts. The main character of another movie was able to cope with difficult issues. This movie had positive effects on viewers.

have more stigma around mental illness. People from these cultures may be less likely to seek treatment.

Many Asian and Asian American cultures place a high value on a family's position in society. Hurting family reputation may cause suicidal thoughts. However, the importance of family may be protective. A fear of letting their families down may prevent suicide attempts.

Religious involvement may lower suicide risk. This could be for many reasons. Religious participation may help create a supportive community. Religious people

People who belong to a religious community may have a lower risk of suicide than those who do not identify with a religion.

may have belief systems that give them a sense of purpose and hope.

SUICIDE LOSS SURVIVORS

Losing someone to suicide is painful. Stigma may cause people to feel isolated while grieving. Friends and family may not know how to offer support.

People may keep the cause of death secret after a suicide. This can lead to feelings of shame. Family members may blame each other for the suicide.

People experience many emotions after losing someone to suicide. They may wonder if they could have prevented the death. This can lead to self-blame. Survivors of suicide loss may unrealistically believe they could have prevented the death.

Suicide loss survivors may experience other long-term effects. They may develop PTSD. They are at an increased risk of suicidal thoughts themselves. Counseling

Survivors of suicide loss may feel shame and guilt.

can help suicide loss survivors. Having support from friends and their community can make a big difference.

CHAPTER FOUR

HOW ARE SUICIDAL FEELINGS TREATED?

Suicidal thoughts can be frightening and dangerous. Thankfully, there are many treatments available. Some have been used successfully for many years. There are also new treatments. Some treatments help with mental health conditions. But it

Therapists can help patients deal with their suicidal thoughts.

is also important to deal with suicidal thoughts directly.

THERAPY

Many mental health conditions are treated with therapy. Treating these conditions may help lessen suicidal thoughts. Therapy can also help people to work on suicidal thoughts directly. There are two common forms of therapy.

The first type is cognitive behavioral therapy (CBT). CBT teaches patients to recognize troubling thoughts and feelings. It gives them coping skills. It teaches them to replace negative thoughts. CBT is an effective treatment for many mental health conditions. CBT can also target suicidal thoughts.

The second type is dialectical behavior therapy (DBT). It helps people with extreme emotions and harmful behaviors. This includes people with ongoing suicidal

Patients learn skills during therapy that help them recognize and replace negative thoughts.

thoughts. DBT patients learn new ways of thinking and coping. DBT also focuses on managing emotions. It has been shown to reduce suicide risk.

Collaborative Assessment and Management of Suicidality (CAMS) is a suicide-specific approach to treatment. CAMS helps patients replace suicidal thoughts. They develop new problem-solving and coping skills.

MEDICATIONS

Medications are often prescribed to treat mental health conditions. Treating these conditions may reduce suicide risk. However, there aren't many medications that directly treat suicidal urges.

Doctors often prescribe antidepressants to treat depression. These can treat other mental health conditions too. Some antidepressants help increase the level

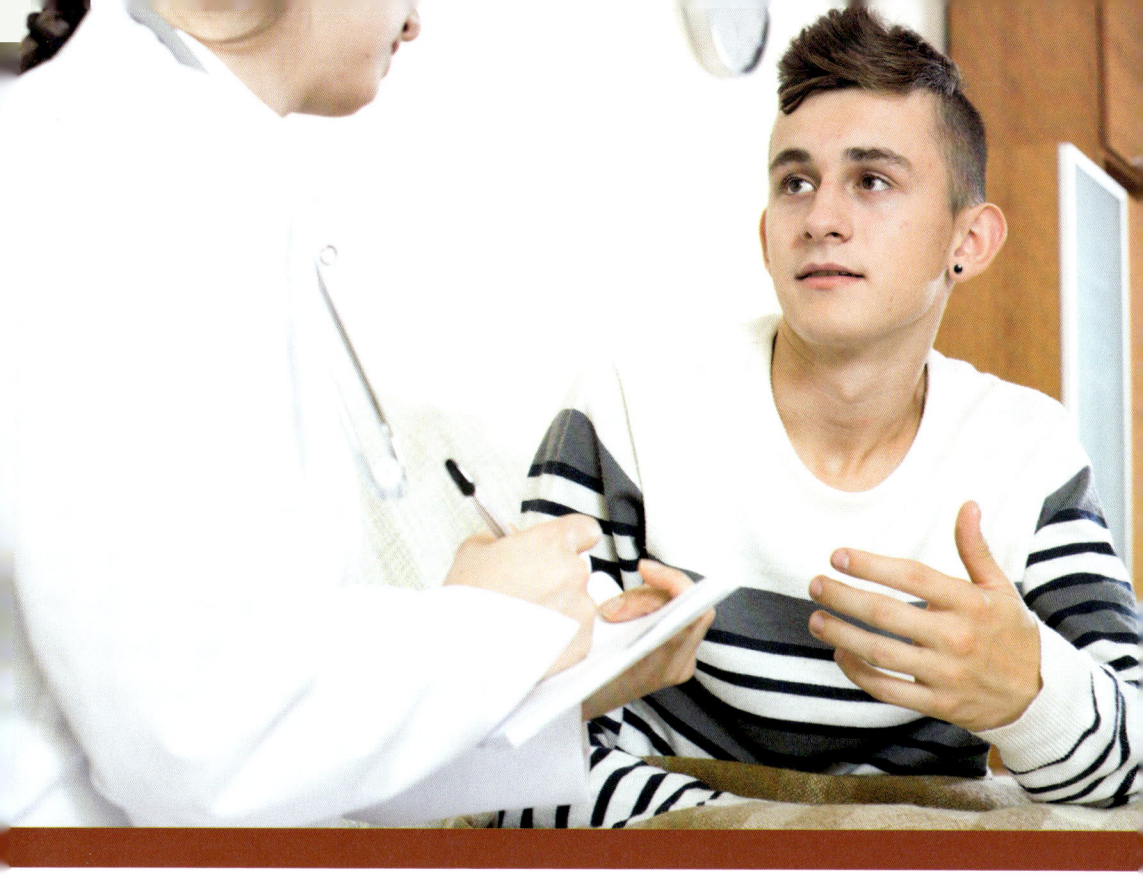

Patients should speak with a doctor if they experience any side effects from medication.

of serotonin available in the brain. This elevates mood.

The relationship between antidepressants and suicide risk is unclear. They lower suicide risk in adults over age twenty-five. But some antidepressants might increase suicidal urges in youth. This occurs only in a small number of these patients.

Medication and therapy are both effective treatments. They may be even more effective when combined. Doctors and patients must work together to find the treatments that work best.

ALTERNATIVE AND INNOVATIVE TREATMENTS

Many other treatments may lessen suicidal urges. The Food and Drug Administration approved the drug esketamine to treat suicidal thoughts in 2019. The drug can reduce symptoms within twenty-four

Doctors may give patients esketamine to help them through a suicidal moment. Esketamine is given as a nasal spray.

hours of the first dose. It may be able to quickly help people experiencing a suicidal moment.

Electroconvulsive therapy (ECT) can also be used to treat suicidal thoughts. ECT uses electrical stimulation of the brain. It was once very dangerous. But it is much safer today. ECT is used when other treatments aren't successful.

Other treatments for depression use brain stimulation. These include magnetic stimulation. Another treatment uses electricity to stimulate a nerve connected to the brain. These treatments may also help reduce suicidal thoughts.

PREVENTION IN HEALTH CARE

Screening can help prevent suicide. Doctors can ask their patients about suicidal thoughts. One screening tool is the Ask Suicide-Screening Questions tool. One study found that this tool could identify

Screening tools can help doctors identify people who are at risk for suicide.

97 percent of youth ages ten to twenty-one who were at risk for suicide.

One study screened all adult emergency room patients. Patients who were found to be at risk worked with a professional. They developed a safety plan together.

A safety plan helps patients who are feeling suicidal. They know who they can reach out to for help. They learn coping methods. They remove means of suicide from their environments. Professionals also made follow-up calls to the patients in the study. These methods decreased suicide attempts by 30 percent over one year.

Technology also plays a role in suicide prevention. An app called MY3 helps people create safety plans. Tec-Tec is a word game app. It teaches people to think negatively about self-harm. It also helps them think more positively about themselves.

The US government approved a new number that responds to mental health crises. The emergency number 988 connects callers to the National Suicide Prevention Lifeline crisis center. It was scheduled to be in full effect by July 2022.

NOW MATTERS NOW

Now Matters Now is an organization that is dedicated to suicide prevention. Its team is made up of mental health professionals and survivors of suicidal thoughts. They share their struggles with mental health and suicidal urges. They also teach people mindfulness and DBT skills. These skills can help people with suicidal thoughts. But they are not replacements for therapy or medication.

The National Suicide Prevention Lifeline connects people struggling with suicidal urges with mental health professionals.

PREVENTION IN SOCIETY

There are many organizations for preventing suicide. Some programs work to reduce stigma. They encourage people to ask for help. Many of these organizations also help suicide attempt survivors and suicide loss survivors. Some fund research on suicide prevention. Some focus on the LGBTQ community. Others focus on people in certain racial or ethnic groups.

Suicide prevention organizations can have a big impact. A young woman named Vicky Powelson lost her father to suicide. She went to walks organized by the American Foundation for Suicide Prevention (AFSP). She was inspired to organize her own walk. She says, "I decided that this fight against suicide was my passion and I was determined to bring awareness and prevention to my community. I would do whatever it took to help in AFSP's mission to reduce the suicide rate 20 percent by 2025."[6]

Suicidal thoughts and suicide continue to be major public health issues. But there is hope for change. Treatments for

NATIONAL SUICIDE PREVENTION MONTH

September is National Suicide Prevention Month. The National Suicide Prevention Lifeline uses the message #BeThe1To. It encourages people to take steps to help people who may have suicidal thoughts. These steps include asking people if they are considering suicide. They also include listening and offering support. People can keep others away from means of attempting suicide. They should follow up and connect people to other resources.

People can wear or display a yellow ribbon as a symbol to raise suicide awareness.

suicidal thoughts can help save lives. So can prevention programs. Programs and individuals can help reduce the stigma around mental health. They can encourage people with suicidal thoughts to get help. These are important steps to help those with suicidal thoughts.

GLOSSARY

gay-straight alliances

school groups that bring together LGBTQ and non-LGBTQ students to build a community and work toward social change

intoxication

the state of being affected by drugs or alcohol

LGBTQ

lesbian, gay, bisexual, transgender, or queer/questioning

neurotransmitter

a chemical that sends messages within the brain and the body

stabilizes

makes something steady and less likely to worsen

stigma

a societal attitude about something that creates shame around it and makes people feel embarrassed to be associated with it

transgender

identifying as a gender that differs from the sex assigned at birth

trauma

an experience that is very disturbing and often causes a serious emotional response

SOURCE NOTES

CHAPTER ONE: WHAT ARE SUICIDAL FEELINGS?

1. Jill Harkavy-Friedman, "Ask Dr. Jill: Does Mental Illness Play a Role in Suicide?" *American Foundation for Suicide Prevention*, February 7, 2020. www.afsp.org.

2. Quoted in Colleen de Bellefonds, "How to Deal with Suicidal Thoughts—From 7 Women Who've Been There," *Women's Health*, September 6, 2018. www.womenshealthmag.com.

CHAPTER TWO: HOW DO SUICIDAL FEELINGS AFFECT PEOPLE?

3. Quoted in Katie Kindelan, "On World Suicide Prevention Day, What 4 Survivors of Suicide Want You to Know," *Good Morning America*, September 9, 2019. www.goodmorningamerica.com.

4. Quoted in Rheana Murray, "What Is It Like to Survive a Suicide Attempt?" *Today*, September 23, 2019. www.today.com.

CHAPTER THREE: HOW DO SUICIDAL FEELINGS AFFECT SOCIETY?

5. Quoted in Tim Fitzsimons, "40 Percent of LGBTQ Youth 'Seriously Considered' Suicide in Past Year, Survey Finds," *NBC News*, July 15, 2020. www.nbcnews.com.

CHAPTER FOUR: HOW ARE SUICIDAL FEELINGS TREATED?

6. Vicky Powelson, "Together We Can," *American Foundation for Suicide Prevention*, August 11, 2020. https://afsp.org.

FOR FURTHER RESEARCH

BOOKS

Matt Chandler, *Understanding Suicide*. Ann Arbor, MI: Cherry Lake, 2020.

Kathy MacMillan, *Understanding Bipolar Disorder*. San Diego, CA: ReferencePoint Press, 2021.

H. W. Poole, *Depression*. Broomall, PA: Mason Crest, 2016.

INTERNET SOURCES

"Mental Health Conditions and Suicide," *American Foundation for Suicide Prevention*, 2021. https://afsp.org.

"Suicide (for Teens)," *TeensHealth from Nemours,* October 2020. https://kidshealth.org.

"Suicide in America: Frequently Asked Questions," *National Institute of Mental Health,* n.d. www.nimh.nih.gov.

WEBSITES

American Foundation for Suicide Prevention
https://afsp.org

The American Foundation for Suicide Prevention offers information about suicide and how to prevent it. It also offers resources for those affected by suicide and suicidal thoughts.

Seize the Awkward
https://seizetheawkward.org

Seize the Awkward offers tools and guidelines for discussing mental health and reducing stigma.

Suicide Awareness Voices of Education (SAVE)
https://save.org

SAVE is one of the first US organizations dedicated to the prevention of suicide. It raises public awareness and educates communities about suicide. SAVE works to equip people with the necessary tools to prevent suicide.

INDEX

age, 13, 44, 46–47, 63, 67
American Foundation for Suicide Prevention (AFSP), 71–72
amygdalae, 29

Born This Way Foundation, 35

Collaborative Assessment and Management of Suicidality (CAMS), 61–62
culture, 53–55

gender, 44, 47–48

hippocampus, 29

lesbian, gay, bisexual, transgender, or queer/questioning (LGBTQ), 48–51, 71

medication
   antidepressants, 11, 62–63
   esketamine, 64–65

National Suicide Prevention Lifeline, 17, 69, 72
Now Matters Now, 69

racial groups, 44–46, 71
risk factors
   access to firearms, 27, 48
   bipolar disorder, 18–19
   bullying, 27
   depression, 18–19, 28, 38, 43, 62, 66
   family history, 26
   schizophrenia, 20
   substance use disorders, 21–24, 37
   trauma, 16, 20, 24–25

safety plans, 67–68
screening tools, 66–67
self-harm, 20, 34, 48, 68
serotonin, 28, 63
stigma, 35–36, 51–52, 54–55, 70, 73
survivors of suicide loss, 55–57, 70–71

therapy
   cognitive behavioral therapy (CBT), 60
   dialectical behavior therapy (DBT), 60–61, 69

warning signs, 37–40

IMAGE CREDITS

Cover: © LaraBelova/iStockphoto
5: © seb_ra/iStockphoto
7: © g-stockstudio/iStockphoto
9: © SDI Productions/iStockphoto
10: © kali9/iStockphoto
13: © SDI Productions/iStockphoto
15: © Lado/Shutterstock Images
19: © Obradovic/iStockphoto
21: © Daisy-Daisy/iStockphoto
23: © RyanKing999/iStockphoto
25: © tillsonburg/iStockphoto
29: © SciePro/iStockphoto
31: © mdurson/iStockphoto
33: © Ben_Gingell/iStockphoto
36: © stockphoto mania/Shutterstock Images
39: © Chainarong Prasertthai/iStockphoto
41: © Rachaphak/iStockphoto
45: © Cesar Fernandez Dominguez/iStockphoto
47: © PeopleImages/iStockphoto
49: © Red Line Editorial
51: © jax10289/Shutterstock Images
55: © No-Te Eksarunchai/Shutterstock Images
57: © Rawpixel.com/Shutterstock Images
59: © KatarzynaBialasiewicz/iStockphoto
61: © dragana991/iStockphoto
63: © JackF/iStockphoto
65: © Neznam/iStockphoto
67: © Wilson Araujo/iStockphoto
70: © ventdusud/iStockphoto
73: © AaronAmat/iStockphoto

ABOUT THE AUTHOR

R. L. Van is a writer and editor living in the Twin Cities, Minnesota. She has written nonfiction books for kids and teens on a variety of topics. In her free time, she enjoys reading, doing crossword puzzles, and playing with her pet cats.